Ginger & the bully

J.E. Simpson

S.E. Simpson

Ginger & the bully

TATE PUBLISHING *& Enterprises*

Published by Tate Publishing & Enterprises, LLC
127 E. Trade Center Terrace | Mustang, Oklahoma 73064 USA
1.888.361.9473 | www.tatepublishing.com

Tate Publishing is committed to excellence in the publishing industry. The company reflects the philosophy established by the founders, based on Psalm 68:11,
"The Lord gave the word and great was the company of those who published it."

Book design copyright © 2011 by Tate Publishing, LLC. All rights reserved.
Cover design by Kenna Davis
Interior design by Stephanie Woloszyn

Published in the United States of America

ISBN: 978-1-61777-795-0
1. Juvenile Fiction / Social Issues / Bullying
2. Juvenile Fiction / Social Issues / Friendship
11.06.20

# Dedication

To my daughters, Rachel and Holly, who have been my inspiration, my supporters, and my audience. Thank you for your encouragement and your belief in me.

To my mom, who was always my mentor, my greatest fan, and my friend. I know that you are smiling down from heaven.

To my Lord, who gave me the dream, the desire, the persistence, and the talent to imagine all the stories and poems over the years.

chapter 1

My name is Lucretia Virginia Ryan, and if you think it's easy to go through life with a name like that, then you probably think doing a no-handed cartwheel is easy. At least I have a nickname that suits me: Ginger. I have red—actually strawberry blonde—hair and little brown freckles dotted across my nose and cheeks. I have almost turquoise-colored eyes, which I think are the only pretty features I have. I'm going into the fourth grade at Chestnut Ridge Elementary School, and if I don't get Mrs. Sabrinski for a teacher, I'll just die. Melody Harper, who has been my best friend since kindergarten, wants to get Mrs. Sabrinski too. We've been together every year. If we aren't together again this year, well, I'll just die over that too. Tomorrow is the Friday before the first day of school. We get to go see who our teachers will be and find out what stuff we need for school. I can't wait!

• • •

"Come on, Mom!" I called from the living room the next afternoon. "Let's go."

"Pipe down, squirt. What's the rush? It isn't like you don't know your way around Chestnut Ridge Elementary blindfolded," said Matt, hitting me on the head with his rolled up *Sports Illustrated* magazine."

"Mom, Matt hit me!"

Matthew Allen Ryan, otherwise known as Matt the Brat, is my older brother. He's in middle school, and he thinks he's so cool. He'll be in eighth grade, and he likes me to think he knows everything. I think he's a jerk. Thank goodness he doesn't look anything like me. He's tall and has dark hair and brown eyes. Maybe he was adopted and his real parents will come looking for him soon.

Just then Mom came into the living room, and she didn't even say anything to Matt for hitting me. "Are you sure you don't want to go to the open house at your school, Matt?" she asked.

"Naw. I know who the eighth-grade teachers are and where their rooms are."

"Do you want to come with us?"

Please say no. Please say no. I wished hard.

"Naw. I'll just hang out here."

Whew! I could breathe again. I didn't want Matt to come. He always makes fun of everything, and he teases me in front of my friends.

"We won't be too long," Mom called. "Ready, Ginger?"

I nodded. I had been ready and waiting for her.

Mom and I just about ran from the car to the little brick school, but when we got inside, we found that we should have taken our time. Kids and parents were all around the tables that had the class lists on them. The fourth and fifth grade tables had the shortest lines, so that was one good thing. Finally it was our turn, and I grabbed the list with Mrs. Sabrinski's name on the top. I quickly scanned the list of names and then read more slowly. There was Melody's name with the H's, so I read on down. Brenda Queen, Mark Reilly, John Roberts, Lauren Sanders. "Mom, I don't see my name," I whispered, elbowing my mother.

"Here it is, sweetie," Mom replied, holding over the paper she had picked up. Sure enough, there it was—Lucretia Ryan. Then I looked at the top of the paper. Ms. Lindell.

"Oh, no, Mom. There must be a mistake. I'm supposed to be in Mrs. Sabrinski's class with Melody."

"I guess they split you up this year, honey. You have Ms. Lindell."

"I can't! I won't go!" I knew my voice was getting louder. That's probably why Mom dropped the papers on the table and steered me out of the way. "Mom, you don't understand. Ms. Lindell is the meanest teacher in the school, probably in the whole state!"

"She can't be that bad," Mom soothed. "Let's just go talk to her. I'm sure she won't bite you."

I trudged along beside my mother, but I wasn't moving very fast. Of all things, I had to see Melody come bouncing out of Mrs. Sabrinski's room with a smile big enough to crack open her face.

"Hi, Ginger. Isn't it great? I got Mrs. Sabrinski." Melody was so cheerful that I felt like kicking her.

"Great, Mel. I didn't."

"Oh, no, Ginger. You got the wicked witch?" I nodded. "Well, I'll see you at recess. We'll still have fun."

That was easy for her to say. She got the nicest teacher on earth, and I got Ms. Grouch of the Universe. How much fun could I possibly have?

All too soon we reached the classroom. I took a deep breath, and Mom grabbed my hand. I guess she was afraid I would run away. That thought did cross my mind. Ms. Lindell stood beside her desk at the far corner, so we had to walk all the way across the room to talk to her. She didn't look too scary. She wore a lavender colored skirt and a flowered shirt and sandals. Her dark hair had been cut short and looked a lot better than the shoulder-length frizzy hair she had last year. She had big brown eyes, the better to see us with, I'm sure. I didn't see any broomstick or pointed black hat, and for that I was grateful.

"Who have we here?" she asked with only the slightest hint of a smile at the corners of her mouth. I don't think I have ever seen her really smile. Maybe she didn't know how. Mom nudged me, but I couldn't get my voice to come out.

"This is Lucretia Ryan," Mom said.

"Ginger," I squeaked. At the mention of "Lucretia," my voice suddenly returned.

"You want to be called Ginger?" Ms. Lindell asked.

"Yes…please," I whispered.

"No problem. Ginger it is. Let me write that down so I don't forget." Then Ms. Lindell told Mom and me what kind of notebooks and things I'd need. She asked me if I had any questions, but I just shook my head.

"She's not usually so shy," Mom said. She said a few more polite things, thanked Ms. Lindell, and led me out of the room. "She seemed nice enough," Mom whispered when we were in the hallway.

"Ugh!" I responded. I was afraid I might never talk in school again. I would probably develop some kind of condition where my mouth wouldn't even open and close right. I'd be the laughing stock of Chestnut Ridge Elementary.

chapter 2

On the first day of school, I heard Matt's alarm go off at 6:00 a.m. I think I heard every owl that hooted and every bullfrog that croaked all night long. I pulled the pillow over my head and tried to pretend it wasn't Monday morning. I tucked the edges of the pillow around my ears, but I could still hear Matt pad down the hall to the bathroom and turn on the shower. Then I heard the hairdryer, but it wasn't on long because Matt doesn't have a whole lot of hair. I must have finally dozed, because the next thing I knew, my alarm was buzzing in my head. I reached up, slapped it off, rolled over, and pulled the covers up to my chin. Why did today have to come? This was going to be the beginning of the worst year of my life, and I wanted to put off the dreaded beginning for as long as possible.

"Ginger, get up!" Mom called from the kitchen.

"Ugh!" I mumbled. I waited a few more minutes then kicked off the covers. I pulled on new turquoise shorts that matched my eyes, a new tee shirt, socks, and new tennis shoes. The only good thing about today was that I got to wear new clothes.

I took my time making my bed, smoothing out every tiny wrinkle. I placed my teddy bear, stuffed cat, and my old Cabbage Patch doll, Miranda Lynette, against my pillows and then rearranged them all twice.

"Ginger, come eat breakfast. Hurry up!" Mom called. I heard a trace of anger in her voice, so I left my doll and animals and shuffled down the hall to the kitchen.

"Pancakes today in honor of the first day of school," Mom announced cheerfully.

"Don't remind me," I grumbled.

"Cheer up, sweetie." Mom handed me a plate with a stack of pancakes.

"I don't feel very well. Maybe I'm coming down with something."

"Nonsense," Mom replied. "You just have school-itis—a bad case of the first-day jitters."

"I think I'll have it every day. I may even die of it."

Mom laughed. "I don't think so. You'll be just fine. Hurry and eat. Then I'll French braid your hair."

I poured syrup over my pancakes and tried to eat, but it was hard to get pancakes past the lump in my throat. For some reason I felt like crying, but I didn't because I didn't want to go to school with red eyes and be called a crybaby. I scraped the pancakes in the trashcan when Mom wasn't looking, rinsed my plate, and left it in the sink. I let Mom braid my hair and even put a bow in it. I wasn't in the mood to care how I looked.

The bus driver must have made it to school in record time. I didn't remember getting to school so fast last year. I waited to be the last one off the bus, and all the little kids thought I was a goddess or something since I didn't trample over them to get off. Mrs. Peterson, the principal, stood inside the front door smiling at all the kids as we came into the school. I tried to smile back, but my lips shook almost as much as my hands did. What I really wanted to do was turn around and run right back out the door as fast as I could. Instead I got caught up in the shuffle of kids moving down the fourth and fifth grade hall and finally ended up in front of room 18, Ms. Lindell's room.

I stopped in the doorway and just looked inside, but I got pushed from behind by Jimmy Bradford, Adam Gordon, and some dorky-looking new boy. Jimmy and Adam hollered, "Move it, Ginger."

I found my name on a desk near the front of the room, and to my horror, the dorky new kid sat next to me. His last name was Ryan too. This *was* going to be a rotten year.

"So you're Lucretia," he said loud enough for everyone in three neighboring counties to hear.

"How'd you know that?" The nametag on my desk said Ginger. Ms. Lindell remembered.

"My name was after yours on the list. Lucretia Ryan, Todd Ryan. I have a photographic memory."

"You have a big mouth." In that instant, I knew Todd Ryan was going to be my lifelong enemy. Great! I not only had the wicked witch of Chestnut Ridge for a teacher, but I was going to have to sit next to the king of creeps too.

Shy little Katie Stevens, who sat behind me, tapped me on the shoulder and whispered, "Just ignore him.

He's a jerk." That was the most I had ever heard her say, but at least maybe I had someone on my side.

• • •

The day didn't get any better. Recess took forever to come, and I couldn't wait to get out and talk to Melody. By the time I got outside, Melody was already playing tag with some kids from her class.

"Hi, Mel. Want to go for a walk?"

"I'm playing tag now, Ginger."

"Can I play?"

"We've already started." I knew when I wasn't wanted, but it hurt that my best friend didn't want me to play. I walked off alone.

"What's the matter, Lucretia? Nobody want to play with you? With a name like that, I don't blame them." It was that new boy, Todd, who felt it was his duty to torment me.

"Don't you have anything better to do?" I asked.

"I'm having fun bugging you."

"Why bother?"

"Because I know a nerd when I see one."

I clamped my teeth together and silently counted to ten, but Todd spoke again by the time I got to number seven. "Couldn't your mama think of a decent name for you? Boy, she must be even dumber than you!"

I was ready to explode, but someone grabbed my arm and a small voice said, "Come on, Ginger. Come play jump rope with me." I turned to see Katie beside me. She flung her brown braids over her shoulders with one hand and tugged on my arm with the other. "Don't pay any attention to him. What does he know? He's just a dumb boy."

"Yeah, run to your little friend!" Todd yelled as we walked off to get a jump rope.

"Don't pay any attention," Katie repeated. "Don't even look at him." She pulled a red-handled jump rope out of the box and handed it to me and then got one for herself.

"Thanks, Katie," I said quietly. Out of the corner of my eye I saw Todd run off to play kickball with Jimmy, Adam, and some fifth grade boys. "I don't know what I ever did to him."

"Nothing. He's the one with a problem."

We swung the ropes behind us and jumped until the whistle blew to end recess.

I wasn't in any hurry to go back into the classroom to sit beside big-mouth Todd Ryan. Why did I have to sit beside him? Why did his name have to be the same as mine anyway?

Social studies was after recess, and I had a hard time concentrating because Todd kept drawing dumb pictures of monsters and animals and writing my name under them. I was so afraid that Ms. Lindell would call on me for something and I'd look like a dummy since I didn't have any idea what she was talking about.

At last the bell rang, and it was time to go home. Thank goodness Todd didn't ride my bus. I sat next to the window, leaned my head against the cool glass of the bottom half, and let loose wisps of hair blow around me. I wished my problems would blow out of the window. Fat chance!

chapter 3

"Mom!" I yelled as soon as I got in the house. "Mom, why in the world did you have to name me Lucretia? You could have named me Mary or Ann or anything. Why Lucretia?"

"What's all this about?" Mom asked, coming from the kitchen and wiping her hands on a dishtowel.

"Lucretia is such an awful name! Why did you do that to me?"

"Sweetheart, you know you were named for my grandmother, the sweetest, gentlest woman on earth."

"You didn't give Matt the name George after Great-grandpa. Wasn't he sweet too?"

"Grandpa was a wonderful man, but Grandma and I always had a special relationship. I wanted to honor her by naming my little girl after her. Now, do you want to tell me what's wrong?"

I told Mom about the new kid with our last name and how mean he'd been to me. I had to keep sniffing, but I told her Melody wouldn't play with me at recess, and then, to my horror, a flood of tears poured down my face. "I...I...hate school...and...and...I...I'm not going back!" Mom pulled me into her arms and just let me cry on her shoulder.

"What's wrong with the squirt?" Matt asked, coming into the room. I didn't look up, but Mom must have given him a dirty look, because I heard him go back the way he came.

When my crying turned back into sniffing, Mom pulled back and looked me in the eye. "You have to go back to school, Ginger," she said. "I think it will probably be best for you to ignore this Todd boy. He must have some problem, or maybe he's angry about moving here or something and he's taking it out on you. If he knows he upsets you, he's going to keep on doing and saying mean things. Just show him that he doesn't bother you. Give it a while, can you?"

I nodded, but I wasn't sure how long I could give it.

"If things don't get better, we'll talk to Ms. Lindell."

"Oh, no! I don't want to do that. Then I'll look like a real baby," I wailed.

"Then just do your best work and ignore Todd."

"I'll try, Mom. I'll go change clothes before I do my homework."

"Homework on the first day?"

"Just a writing assignment."

I tried to tiptoe down the hall so Matt wouldn't hear me, but he must have had his ear right on his door. Before I could get inside my room, he yanked open his door and slid down the hall in his sock feet. "Maybe this boy has a crush on you, Ginger."

"Shut up, Matt."

"Or maybe he's a child ax murderer and you're his next victim." Matt wrapped his hands around my throat, pretending to choke me.

"Leave me alone!" I yelled, pulling at his hands.

"You'd better learn how to protect yourself, Ginger. What if he tries to sneak in your room at night and—"

"Mom! Matt won't leave me alone." I stomped on his shoeless foot, and he jumped back with a shriek.

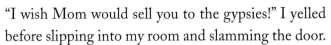

"I wish Mom would sell you to the gypsies!" I yelled before slipping into my room and slamming the door.

I hung up my new school clothes and put on my favorite old pair of jean shorts and a faded summer camp tee shirt. I flopped across the bed and thought about my rotten day and my rotten brother.

I was just finishing my homework when Mom called us to dinner. I waited until I heard Matt come out of his room and head for the kitchen before I opened my door. I didn't want to be alone with him after stomping on his foot. Matt always got even.

Mom must have told Matt to leave me alone, because he was almost polite to me at dinner. Since Daddy died four years ago, Mom has had to be mother and father to us. Matt and I both know it's tough for her, so every now and then he tries to act grown up to help her out. Maybe he'd forget about getting even with me. I couldn't count on that, though.

After dinner, Matt cleared the table and took out the trash while I washed the dishes. I pretended one plate was Todd's face, and I scrubbed as hard as I could until I was afraid that I would scrub the painted flowers right off.

"Ease up on the plate, squirt. If you break it, you might cut an artery or something and bleed to death.

We wouldn't want that to happen, would we?" Matt had just come in from hauling the trashcans to the end of the driveway, and he was still breathing hard.

"Why didn't you jump in one of those cans so you could take a ride to the dump tomorrow?"

"I was afraid I'd run into you there," he answered, squeezing the back of my neck.

"Leave me alone, Matt."

"Matthew, will you come here, please?" Mom called from another part of the house. Matt made a face at me and gave my neck one last squeeze before starting in the direction of Mom's voice. Honestly, I don't think boys ever grow up.

chapter 4

I wish I could say that things got better, but my life kept going downhill. Todd was still drawing stupid pictures of me in class, but I forced myself to concentrate on whatever Ms. Lindell was saying. I was still afraid to raise my hand in class because I didn't want everyone to laugh at me if I said the wrong thing.

During science on Thursday, I must have looked like I knew the answer because Ms. Lindell called on me, and I didn't even have my hand up.

"Ginger, what do you call the place where an animal lives?"

My heart stopped beating. Honest! Then when it started again with a thud, I thought for sure that everyone in the room heard it. It felt like the bottom dropped out of my stomach, and for a second I was afraid I was going to throw up. I turned a little to my left because if I was going to throw up, I wanted it to be all over Todd. I looked up, and Ms. Lindell was still looking at me and waiting.

"A habitat?" I squeaked.

"That's exactly right," Ms. Lindell replied. Her eyes seemed to soften a bit, but she didn't smile. Maybe she was afraid she'd be struck by lightning if she smiled. "Can you tell us anything about this animal's habitat?" she asked, pointing to a picture of a beaver on the wall.

I couldn't believe she was still calling on me. What did I ever do to her? I gulped and then took a deep breath. I loved science, so I looked into Ms. Lindell's face and pretended no one else was in the room. My voice was shaky at first, but I told her everything I knew about beavers. I breathed a sigh of relief when I finished, and Katie tapped me on the shoulder and whispered, "Good job." I nodded a thank you to her.

I ignored Todd's hiss, "What are you, some kind of encyclopedia?"

During math, I had to keep wrapping my arm around my paper because Todd kept trying to peek at my answers. "I bet you don't know the answers anyway," Todd said when he couldn't see what I had written on my paper. It was going to be a long year.

Friday was the worst day ever. At recess, Katie had to stay in to finish her math, so I was hoping I could play with Melody and her friends from her class. Melody was supposed to come to my house to play on Saturday, and I was looking forward to things being like they used to be.

Melody's class was already outside by the time our class made it out the door. She was playing with all the girls she used to call stuck up last year. It was just my luck that Todd pushed his way through the crowd of kids to be right behind me.

"Can't you move any faster, Lucretia? Have you got on concrete shoes?" He shoved me hard, and I stumbled into Jimmy Bradford.

"Move it, Ginger—I mean, Lucretia!" he shouted. I'm sure half the playground heard.

"Where's your little friend, Lucretia?" Todd asked. "Poor Lucretia only has one friend."

I tried to ignore him, but I felt like sticking my foot out and telling Todd to have a nice trip. I raced over to

Melody's group, happy to be away from boys. I didn't know that Todd, Jimmy, and Adam followed me until they started pretending to stumble into each other.

"Hi, Mel," I called. "Can I play with you guys?"

"Hi, Mel," Todd mocked in a high, squeaky voice. "Can I play with you guys?" I tried to pretend he didn't exist, but he kept on. "Of course you can't play with them, Lucretia. They don't let nerds play with them."

"Go away, Todd," I said between clenched teeth. "Can I play?" I asked Melody again.

"We've already started, Ginger."

"So? You're just playing tag. Can't I join?"

"Can't I join?" Todd whined. Melody and her friends laughed.

"Where's your little friend?" Melody asked.

"You mean Katie?"

"Yeah, I forgot the little mouse's name."

"What's wrong with you, Melody? Why are you being so mean?"

"I just want to play with Lauren, Sarah, and Sherri, that's all."

"What about tomorrow? Are you still coming over?"

"Uh, I don't know, Ginger. I was hoping that I could go over to Lauren's house."

"But we made plans a long time ago."

Just then, Lauren ran over and looped her arm through Melody's. "Let's play," she said.

"Melody," I said.

"Melody," Todd echoed.

"Not now, Ginger," Melody called over her shoulder as she started off with Lauren.

"Well, I don't want you to come over to my house ever again, Melody Harper."

"Oh, boo hoo hoo!" Todd said, and Jimmy and Adam rubbed their eyes and pretended to cry. I heard Melody and her friends laughing as I ran toward the school. Todd yelled, "Don't bother telling Ms. Lindell! The dragon lady won't have any pity on you!"

I ran as fast as I could and tried hard not to cry. My eyes were so blurry that I almost bumped into Katie when I reached the door. She had finished her math and was on her way out.

"What's wrong, Ginger?"

I sniffed and told her what happened. She patted my arm and said, "Don't worry, Ginger. Melody has gotten to be just like those other girls, and Todd is just a creep. Don't even think about them." After a minute of silence, she said, "I'm your friend, aren't I?"

"Of course you are, Katie. You are a great friend." And I meant it. We walked inside together and decided to go to the library to read until recess was over. Boy, was I glad it was Friday!

chapter 5

When I pulled open the front door of the house, I felt like sneaking back down the walk and off into the sunset. Matt the Brat was giving Mom a hard time, and I hated to hear them argue. I knew that later Matt would take his anger out on me.

"Matthew, I told you before that you cannot go to Bryan's tonight. I have to run over to one of my classmate's houses for a short study group session. I need you to stay here with Ginger." Mom used to teach school a long time ago, but she quit when Matt was born, so now she's just a mom, except that she's been taking classes so she can teach again.

"Why do you have to do that tonight? Why can't you take the squirt with you?"

"I can't do that. We have an exam on Monday, and some of us just want to get together for a few minutes to make sure we're ready. I'll only be gone a couple of hours at the most."

I felt worse about the whole idea than Matt did, I'm sure. Mom didn't leave us often, but I hated getting left home with Matt, especially if he was going to be in a bad mood.

We had a quick early dinner, and then Mom had to leave. I ran around the house making sure all the doors were locked before even starting the dishes, even though Mom had checked all the doors herself. Matt hung around the kitchen, making me nervous, so I tried to talk to him in the hope of gaining some brotherly advice—for whatever it was worth.

"Matt, what would you do if some kid kept picking on you?"

"I'd bash his face in."

"Come on, Matt. Would you say anything back to him or ignore him?"

"I'd karate chop him across the neck and then ignore him."

"You're no help."

I dried the last dish and reached to hang up the towel when Matt grabbed my arm. "Come on, Ginger. I'll teach you some moves." He jerked my arm almost out of its socket, started kicking, and made grunting noises.

"Let go of me, you idiot! You almost broke my arm!" I jerked my arm free and rubbed it.

"I'm just trying to show you how to get mean."

"I'm sure you're an expert in meanness, but you don't know anything about karate. I should have known better than to try to talk to you." I stomped off to my room and flopped across my bed to read a book. Matt returned to his rat hole of a room and turned his crazy music up full blast. I stretched my leg out as far as I could so I could kick my door shut. The music was still so loud that my teeth rattled. "I hope you go deaf!" I yelled, but I knew Matt couldn't hear me.

I couldn't concentrate on my book, even though it was a good mystery, so I decided to rearrange my room instead. I couldn't budge the bed or dresser, so I dragged and pushed the bookcase, desk, and toy box around until the toy box with my teddy sitting on it was under the window, my desk was against the wall just inside the door, and the bookcase that I had to unload and then reload was near my closet.

After all that work I needed a bath, so I tiptoed down the hall, though I shouldn't have bothered. Matt wouldn't have heard a tornado if it came down the hall and tore through his room. I soaked in the bubbles until they all died and then dried off with a fluffy towel. I pulled on my favorite pajamas with the cats on them. I brushed my teeth and even flossed them. Back in my room, I moved my stuffed cat and Miranda Lynnette, folded back my blue and white flowered comforter, and pulled down the blanket and sheet. My good old teddy bear looked lonely on the toy box, so I snatched him off and hugged him tightly. Mom and Daddy gave Teddy to me when I was just a tiny baby, and I planned to keep him forever. Teddy and I crawled beneath the covers and waited for sleep to come.

All of a sudden Matt's music stopped, and that made the house seem strangely quiet. When I heard Matt's footsteps get close to my room, I squeezed my eyes shut and pretended to be asleep. I started to fake a snore, but since I don't usually snore, I figured that would give me away. I could feel Matt standing in my doorway, but I still didn't open my eyes. I couldn't hear him move or breathe, so I opened one eye just a crack and saw him run his hand through his brown hair until it stood almost straight up in the air, like the hair on a cat's back when a dog gets close to it. I imagined Matt the cat trying to claw his way up a tree to get away from a huge German Shepherd. All of a sudden, I wanted to laugh, but I bit my tongue until I thought it would drop off.

"Ginger, you awake?" Matt asked as quietly as he could ever make himself speak.

"Mmmm," I moaned.

He came close to my bed and called my name again. I stretched and wiggled and mumbled, "What do you want?"

He sat on the edge of my bed and ran his hand through his hair again. This time I did laugh. "What's so funny?" he asked.

"You are when you do that with your hair." Since Matt didn't think his hair was at all funny, I didn't say anything else. I just waited for him to tell me why he came into my room, since he so rarely leaves his own cave to grace me with his presence.

"Ginger, is somebody really bothering you at school?"

"Yeah." I didn't want to say much because I didn't want him to tease me.

"Listen, I'm sorry I wasn't much help. Who is the kid?"

"Todd Ryan."

"What's he doing?"

I told Matt some of the things Todd had said and done and how I tried to ignore him but that didn't work either.

"Have you talked to the teacher?"

"Are you kidding?" I exploded. "I couldn't talk to her. Ms. Lindell is the meanest teacher in the world."

"Sounds like she's just the one to get Todd for you. At least maybe she'd change his seat."

"I can't tell, Matt. Todd would know I told, and he'd make my life even more miserable—if that's possible." Suddenly I felt like crying. "I wish Daddy were here," I whispered.

"Me too," Matt agreed, patting my shoulder, "but I think you've got to take care of this Todd character yourself, or he'll keep on bullying you."

"What am I going to do?"

"Do you want me to bash his face in?"

I laughed and shook my head no.

"Then let me think about it. Try not to worry. He'll probably get tired of tormenting you soon."

I didn't think so, but I appreciated what Matt was trying to do. It wasn't usually like him to be nice or helpful. "Thanks," I said.

"G'night, Ginger."

"G'night, Matt."

chapter 6

The air was crisp and cool, and the leaves that had dropped off the trees crunched underfoot. I loved the crackly sound the leaves made when I walked on them. The weather was just right for Halloween, which is my favorite holiday next to Christmas. My birthday doesn't count because it's not actually a holiday. Mom was supposed to finish making my costume today, and I couldn't wait to get into the house to try it on. I was going to be my favorite animal—a cat. My costume wasn't going to be a black leotard and tights with pinned on tail and ears. No, sireee! Mom had bought furry black material and was making a whole suit. A hood with ears, a tail, and paws were made right on to it.

I heard Mom's sewing machine as soon as I pushed open the front door. "Hi, Mom!" I yelled.

"Hi, baby. Come in the sewing room."

I dropped my book bag right where I was standing and raced to the tiny spare bedroom that Mom called her sewing room.

"I just finished," she said and held up the costume. "What do you think?"

"Gosh, Mom, it's great." I couldn't stop running my fingers through the fur.

"Let's try it on." Mom helped me slip the costume on over my clothes. "We'll paint on a black nose and whiskers, and you'll be all set."

I dashed down the hall to the bathroom so I could look in the full-length mirror. If I hadn't been so big, I'd have looked just like a cat. I loved the costume. I started back to the sewing room when I heard panting behind me and then a loud "Ruff, ruff!"

Before I could turn around, something grabbed my leg.

"Ahhh!" I screamed.

"Ruff! I got the giant kitty in one leap."

"Matt, you idiot. Let go of me before you tear my costume."

"Giant talking kitty. Must kill giant talking kitty." His grip on my leg tightened until I lost my balance and fell backward to the floor on top of him.

"Help! Giant kitty fell on me."

"Giant kitty claw mean, ugly dog," I said and then hissed and raised my "paw" as if to scratch his face.

"No, no. Good kitty," Matt said, patting the top of my head extra hard.

"Ow!"

"What are you two doing?" Mom stuck her head out into the hallway.

"He knocked me down," I replied.

"Come on, Ginger. Let's put the costume away before it gets ruined."

I pulled away from Matt and said, "Trot back to your doghouse, mean, ugly dog."

Mom shook her head. She looked like she was disgusted with both of us.

"I love the costume, Mom. It's super!" I wrapped my paws around her waist and hugged her tight.

"I'm glad you like it, sweetie. It's done just in time for your school party tomorrow."

"I can't wait!"

She helped me take off the costume, folded it, and put it in a bag for me. "You'd better get your homework done now while I fix dinner," she said.

I trudged out to where I had dropped my book bag and shuffled back to my room to do my math and spelling. I had to shut my door and put on my earmuffs because Matt's so-called music was blasting down the hall.

• • •

At one thirty the next afternoon, Ms. Lindell let us change for the party. Katie and I hurried to the bathroom to get into our costumes. Melody and her friends were putting the finishing touches on their costumes. Lauren was a cheerleader and had on a short skirt and a sweater and wore bright red lipstick smeared over her lips. Sarah was a princess with a lopsided glittery crown on her head. She wore a long, silky, pink dress and pink lipstick. I guess Sherri was supposed to be a model or something. Her hair stuck up everywhere, and her eyelids were covered with blue eye shadow. She wobbled around in high heels. Melody was Miss America with a sash and a fake fur wrap. She had on eye shadow *and* lipstick. They all looked like they had just stepped out of the pages of some science fiction fashion magazine, but they thought they looked glamorous.

"Move out of our way," Lauren said, pushing past Katie and me. "I bet these two are going to be some kind of animal or angel or something," she said over her shoulder to the other girls.

"Probably skunks," Sherri said, and they all laughed.

I wanted to tell Sherri that I hoped she fell off those stilts she was wearing and broke an ankle, but I didn't want to start a fight and miss my party. Katie and I did wait until they were completely out of the bathroom before we changed—me into my cat costume and Katie into her rabbit costume. We pushed the bathroom door open just a crack to make sure the snooty makeup wearers weren't around before we made a mad dash for room 18.

There were the usual ballerinas, princesses, pirates, and Draculas wandering about the room, but no one had a great costume like mine. Nearly all the kids told me how much they liked my costume, and I meowed my thank yous.

Then someone with a cardboard box over his head turned around. It was Todd! He was a walking television. The front of the box had a square cut out that let Todd's face show through, and there were knobs along the side. He looked at me and burst out laughing. "Look at the kitty!" he called. "Maybe we can catch it in a big trap." He moved toward me. I backed up until I felt the bookcase dig into my behind. "We should put this big kitty in the big litter box on the playground." He laughed at his stupid joke and pulled my arm. I was afraid he would rip my wonderful costume.

"Let go of me!" I cried, jerking free. I hissed and raised cat claws.

"Oooh! This is a mean cat. Maybe it has rabies. We need to shoot it."

"Where is your 'off' button?" I asked, reaching for one of the knobs on the box.

"Paws off!" Todd shouted. He grabbed my arm and began to twist it. Before tears came into my eyes, Ms. Lindell clapped her hands and called us to line up for the parade around the school. "What a dumb costume, Lucretia. I bet the whole school will have a good laugh," Todd said before turning around and heading for the line of kids at the door.

Suddenly I didn't feel like doing the parade. I didn't feel like doing anything. Halloween was ruined.

"Come on, Ginger," Katie prodded. "Let's go. Don't listen to that creep. I think yours is the best costume in the room."

"Thanks, Katie." I didn't feel much better.

"Your costume is really neat. Anybody can do what Todd did for a costume."

"I guess you're right, Katie. You don't have to be a genius to stick a box over your head."

"That's right."

"I just wish there really was a button to turn Todd off."

"Me too." Katie giggled. We hurried to get in the line that had already started down the hall to join the rest of the school for a parade.

After the parade, we had a party in our room, and Ms. Lindell—for once in her life—let us sit anywhere we wanted. Katie and I sat at the back reading table with a few other girls. I was so relieved that I didn't have to suffer through the party next to Todd.

I had brought in decorated cookies that Mom had made, and we had chips and pretzels, candy, and juice. Todd was trying to eat with the box still over his head, and all the boys thought he was hilarious. When he spilled his juice all over his desk and the floor, Ms. Lindell blew up.

"Todd Ryan!" she yelled. "Take that box off now, and clean up that mess." Ms. Lindell hollered so loud that I looked up to see if the light fixtures were shaking. Todd threw the box down and jumped out of his chair. I'd never seen him move so fast. Katie kicked me under the table, and I had to put my hand over my mouth to keep my laughter inside.

• • •

Later in the evening, I was all ready to go trick-or-treating. My costume was on, I had cat whiskers painted on my face, and I had my flashlight and jack-o-lantern to stuff all my goodies in. I could hardly wait, except I had to wait for Mom to finish cleaning up the kitchen.

"Are you ready yet, Mom?" I asked.

"Almost. I'm hurrying."

Just then the doorbell rang. I didn't hear anyone say "trick or treat." I only heard small voices screaming. I ran to the front door in time to see three little kids running in terror down our front walk, their costumes flapping behind them.

"What in the world—" I began as Matt turned away from the door to face me. "Ahhh!" I couldn't help but yell. Matt had painted his face white except for black around the eyes. He had fangs in his mouth and fake blood dripping from his chin. What there was of his hair was sticking straight up on his head, held in place with some slimy, gooey gel. "Mom!" I shrieked. "Matt just scared off some little kids, and they didn't even get any candy."

"Aha," he said, "the more for me, my giant kitty." He came at me walking stiff-legged with his hands stretched out toward my throat.

"Mom. Help!"

"Matthew, what on earth are you doing?" Mom asked.

"Just having a little Halloween fun," he said in his slow, deep monster voice.

"Maybe I should just set the candy outside. You'll scare everyone off."

"That's the whole idea."

"You're impossible, Matthew. Come on, Ginger. We'd better get going, or you won't get any treats. Matt will probably have all these eaten by the time we get home, so you won't get anything here either."

Mom drove me around to the houses of people she knew and inspected all my candy before I ate any of it. She does stuff like that to protect me, she says. I guess that's good.

When we drove into our driveway, I noticed that there were no lights on in the house. "Mom, he's up to something. He's going to jump out and scare us. I'm not going in there."

"Where do you think he's hiding?"

"Probably behind the front door."

"I've got an idea." She reached into the backseat and pulled out the ugliest, scariest mask I had ever seen. "Let's sneak around to his bedroom window and make a noise. When he comes into his room, we'll shine your flashlight up so he sees this in the window," she said, holding up the mask.

We got out of the car and quietly closed the doors. Then we ran all the way around the house to stand outside Matt's window. Mom pulled the ugly mask over her head and loudly knocked on the window frame. She positioned the flashlight so that the light shone only on her head. I ran around to peek in another window; I didn't want to miss any of this! Before Matt could reach for his light switch, he saw Mom's ugly face—I mean the ugly mask—at the window.

"Ahhhh!" he screamed. "Help!"

I collapsed into laughter. Mom yanked off the mask and yelled, "Gotcha!" She and I ran to the front door as Matt angrily snatched it open. "Mom, how could you?" he asked. "I almost had a stroke."

"I thought you liked tricks," Mom replied, pulling Matt to her in a hug. "I bet you scared off all our trick-or-treaters."

"Only the dumb little ones," he said.

"Serves you right, then," I said.

Matt reached for me, but Mom quickly stepped in between us. "It's time to get ready for bed now," she said in her no-nonsense voice.

I shuffled down the hall to my room, smiling to myself. Scaring Matt was better than all the treats I received—almost. Like I said, Halloween is one of my favorite holidays.

chapter 7

Todd continued to bug me, and I continued to feel like an ant that tried to keep from getting stepped on. The more Todd bugged me, the harder I worked on my schoolwork until I was getting As on almost all my papers. I guess I was trying to prove to myself that I really was good at something. I wasn't as worthless as Todd wanted me to believe I was.

When I walked into the classroom one crisp November morning, I saw a strange girl sitting in the back row. She kept her head down, so I couldn't tell what she looked like except for her long, shiny, very dark hair. After the pledge and the morning announcements, Ms. Lindell introduced the girl.

"Boys and girls," she said, "we have a new member of our class. She has lived in India and in England, and we're happy that she is living here now and going to our school. Her name is Camilla Bhakki, and I'm sure you will all make her feel welcome. Now, let's take out our language arts books and turn to page 62."

Before reaching into my desk for my book, I glanced toward the back of the room. Camilla looked up, and for a few seconds our eyes locked. I smiled, and the edges of her lips curved up slightly. She had skin the color of coffee with lots of milk in it—the way mom fixes coffee for me on the very rare occasions she lets me have any—and dark-brown eyes. I thought she was beautiful. I hoped she would be my friend.

At recess time I whispered to Katie, and then we both headed toward Camilla's corner of the room as everyone else hurried for the door. "Hi. I'm Ginger," I said, "and this is Katie. Would you like to play with us?" Camilla nodded, and we started outside.

"Hey!" Todd yelled as soon as our feet hit the playground. "Look guys! Lucretia has a new friend.

She needs all the friends she can get—even if it is a weird foreigner."

That did it! I'd been taking all this abuse from Todd and trying to ignore it, but I wasn't going to let him make this poor, scared new girl feel rotten too.

"Todd Ryan," I said, "you are the nastiest, meanest human being on the face of this earth. Camilla hasn't done a single thing to you—and neither have I for that matter—so just lay off!"

"Whoa! Lucretia can talk, and she seems mad."

"My name is Ginger, and you can take a long walk off a short pier." My hands were beginning to shake, so I said softly, "Come on, Camilla and Katie. Let's go somewhere else."

We figured Todd, Adam, and Jimmy would bother us if we played close by, so we just walked around the playground and talked. "You have beautiful hair," I said to Camilla.

"Thank you," she replied, "but I think yours is such a pretty color." She spoke with a trace of an accent.

"How long have you lived here?" I asked.

"We've been in America for three years, but we just moved to Chestnut Ridge. My father is a doctor, and he joined a new practice here."

"Where did you live before?" Katie asked.

"I lived in India for four years and in England for two years before coming here. My mother is English. We stayed with her family for two years while my father was doing some special work in London."

"How neat!" I said. "I've only lived here for my whole life."

"I lived in Georgia for seven years before we moved here," Katie said. I didn't realize that last year had been Katie's first year at Chestnut Ridge Elementary. I just figured that we were never in the same class. No wonder she was quiet; she hadn't made many friends yet either.

We walked and talked and even laughed a little. Camilla stopped abruptly and looked at me. "You are a very nice, happy, fun kind of person. Your name suits you."

"I wish my mother had named me Ginger instead of the awful name she gave me," I replied.

"Lucretia's not a bad name," Camilla said, and I wrinkled up my nose, "but I like Ginger better."

"Can we call you Cam?" I asked. "Camilla is a great name, but it's kind of long and formal."

"Sure." Camilla giggled. "Just don't let my mother hear you."

We laughed and walked until the whistle blew to end recess. Since we were at the far edge of the playground, we ended up at the back of the line, which was fine with me, because Todd and his buddies were near the front. As we filed past Ms. Lindell into the classroom, she touched my arm and whispered, "It was nice of you to be friendly with Camilla." I just nodded and walked to my desk. I wasn't just doing my good deed for the day. I had made a new friend.

chapter 8

The next day at recess, Cam, Katie, and I hardly got out the door before Melody, Lauren, Sherri, and Sarah swooped down upon us. They all had their hair fixed the same—high side ponytails with white bows. Their lips looked strangely bright, and I wondered if Mrs. Sabrinski minded if her students wore lipstick.

"Who's your new friend?" Melody asked me.

"This is Camilla. Camilla, meet Melody, Lauren, Sherri, and Sarah," I introduced and pointed to each girl in turn.

"Do you want to play with us?"

"I guess we—" Katie started to say.

"We meant Camilla," Lauren said. "You two probably wouldn't be interested."

"Why not?" I asked. "We can all play together."

"I don't think so," Lauren said, grabbing Camilla's arm. She raised her head, nose in the air, and pulled Camilla away.

"I hope it doesn't rain," I whispered to Katie, "or Lauren will drown with her nose stuck up in the air like that."

Katie giggled and ran over to the jump ropes. I followed her and pulled a rope out of the box. I really didn't feel like jumping rope. I felt like running inside the building and crawling inside my desk—if only I'd fit. The lump in my throat felt as big as a baseball. I wanted to yell and be angry at Cam and those mean girls, but instead I struggled not to cry.

Did I have horns growing out of my head? Did I smell bad? Why did girls like Melody and Cam not want to be my friend or even play with me? I tried to ignore the sad, empty feeling that crept over me. I sniffed so hard I thought my ears would pop and gave Katie a shaky smile. "We had a new friend for one day. I guess she'd rather be with the glamour girls."

"If that's the way she wants to be, we don't need her!" Katie could be so sensible. She grabbed my hand that was not clutching the red-handled jump rope and led me over to the blacktop where we could jump in peace.

It was a more or less peaceful recess since Todd had to stay inside because he had gotten his name on the board with three checks after it. When the whistle blew to end recess, Katie and I threw our ropes into the box and ran to get in line. When Camilla walked over to our line, her hair was arranged in a familiar side ponytail. As the line started moving inside the building, Camilla reached up and pulled the ribbon out of her hair and shook her head, freeing her long, dark hair.

I walked quickly to my desk, sat down, and reached for my social studies notebook. Out of the corner of my eye, I spotted something dark. I turned and saw Camilla standing at the edge of my chair. "I didn't want to go with them," she whispered hurriedly. "I had a lot more fun with you and Katie."

"Camilla, take your seat, please," Ms. Lindell barked out.

I smiled at Camilla and nodded my head before she rushed to sit in her own seat. I couldn't believe Camilla would risk the wrath of the wicked witch. She must be a true friend indeed!

Todd was his usual nasty self during social studies, but I didn't pay any attention to him. Either I was getting very good at ignoring him, or else I was so happy that Cam wanted to be my friend that I didn't care what he did. I even raised my hand to answer a question. Boy, was Ms. Lindell surprised!

A three thirty, Ms. Lindell handed each one of us a brown-colored envelope as we walked out the door. Report cards. I was a little scared to see mine, but I thought I had pretty good grades. "Boys and girls, tuck these into your book bags and wait until you get home to open them," Ms. Lindell ordered.

I wasn't sure I could wait. I might have to peek at mine on the bus. When she called my name, I leaped out of my seat so fast that I almost tripped on Todd's foot that just happened to be sticking out in the way. He got a mean kind of smile on his face and whispered, "Watch out, clumsy! Bet you got all Fs."

All the way home on the bus, I sat with my hands on my book bag, playing with the zipper. I was itching to reach inside for that report card, but I was afraid that Witch Lindell—I mean, Ms. Lindell—might have some supernatural power. She'd probably be able to *feel* that I opened my report card on the bus and make a hand come out of the envelope to grab me.

As soon as I hopped off the bus, I ran like a jaguar up the gravel driveway and the sidewalk. I pushed open the front door and heard Mom saying, "I know you can do better in social studies and language arts, Matthew. Your other grades are good, but I want to see improvement in these two."

"Aw, Mom, social studies and language arts are so boring."

"It's up to you to find a way to get interested in them. Maybe a little less music and TV will create an interest."

"Mom!"

"Matthew, I want to see better grades next time."

Matt stomped off to his room, and I knew right away that I didn't want to be alone with him at any time in the near future. Suddenly I was a little afraid to look at my grades. What if they weren't as good as I expected? I didn't want Mom to yell at me. I was so lost in my thoughts that I nearly jumped out of my skin when she spoke to me.

"Hi, baby," she said. "I didn't hear you come in."

"Hi, Mom."

"Did you get your report card?"

I nodded and reached for the zipper on my book bag. "I really worked hard, Mom." I thought I'd better say that just in case my grades weren't very good.

"I know you did, sweetie. Let's see."

I pulled the envelope out, opened it, and slowly removed the paper inside. Mom looked at it over my shoulder. "That's great, Ginger!" she exclaimed. "You did a super job!" I had gotten all As, except for a B in handwriting. I was so happy that I gave Mom a great big bear hug and danced around her. I bet Melody and her snooty friends didn't do that well. "I'm so proud of you," Mom gasped when she was able to breathe again. "We'll make ice cream sundaes tonight to celebrate!"

"Oh boy! I'll go do my homework now. I want to keep getting As." I raced down the hall to my room, forgetting all about Matt until I heard him mock, "I want to keep getting As." I didn't even tell him to shut his big mouth because, to tell the truth, I was afraid he'd come out and hit me or try one of his made-up karate moves again. I decided, for once, to ignore him the way I tried to ignore Todd at school.

After dinner, Mom scooped vanilla ice cream into bowls. I dripped chocolate syrup onto mine and topped it with whipped cream and a cherry. "Mmmm," I mumbled as the first spoonful slid down my throat."

"It's a good thing you got all those As, Ginger, so we could have this delicious treat," Matt said in a sarcastic voice.

"Maybe if you'd get all As, we could have a double treat." I just had to say something back. So much for ignoring him. Now the war was on.

"Eighth grade is just a wee bit tougher than fourth grade," Matt said.

"Eighth grade is tough for you since you're in eighth grade. Fourth grade is tough for me since I'm in fourth grade. Makes sense," I answered.

"Any dummy can get As in fourth grade."

"Yeah, well, did you?"

"I can't remember."

"Well, what kind of dummy are you?"

"Children, that's enough," Mom broke in. "Let's just enjoy our treat—for whatever reason. I'm very proud of you both."

Matt looked across the table at me, and his eyes seemed to say "so there!" I felt like flinging a spoonful of gooey ice cream in his face, but I didn't want to waste a single bite. Also Mom was sitting beside me, so flinging ice cream would not be a smart move. There are many times that I wish I were an only child!

chapter 9

The next day at school was the same as usual. Every day I hoped Todd was just a nightmare, but every day he proved to be real. I was still feeling good about my report card, so I didn't let him bother me too much.

"How was your report card, Lucretia?" He sneered as we were emptying our book bags and putting books away.

"Just fine, thank you, and yours?"

"Probably better than yours."

I wanted to tell him that an earthworm could probably have done better than he did. Did he really think that I hadn't seen all the Ds and all the red marks on his papers? Instead, I just shrugged my shoulders.

I tried to write neater so maybe I could get an A in handwriting too, but sometimes I had to write fast so I would get finished with my work. I usually had enough homework all by itself without adding unfinished class work to it.

When everyone else got ready for recess, I took my time putting my books and papers away and pulling on my jacket. I was hoping Todd would bolt out the door and be far enough away on the playground that he wouldn't be able to bother me.

"Come on, Ginger!" Katie called. "We'll miss all of recess."

"I'm coming."

"How did you guys do on your report cards?" Cam asked as we walked down the hall to the door by the playground.

"I got a B in PE, handwriting, and social studies, but As in the rest," Katie answered.

"I got a B- in math and a B in handwriting, language arts, and PE," Cam said. "Boy, were my parents mad about the math."

"A B- isn't bad," Katie said.

"It's a disgrace at my house," Cam replied glumly. "My parents think I should get all As like my older sister, Dilara. She's a brain. She'll probably be a doctor like my dad."

"Most of those grades are from your old school, Cam," I said. "I bet you'll do even better here."

"How did you do, Ginger?" Katie asked.

"I did fine." I didn't want to seem like I was bragging, so I didn't tell them my actual grades until they dragged it out of me.

Outside, we searched for an unused ball that we could bounce and toss to each other. I heard Todd's voice from across the playground. "There's dumb Lucretia. Hey, everybody, Luceretia got all Fs on her report card."

By this time he had run close enough to hear us, so Camilla said, "She's a lot smarter than you."

"What do you know? You're an alien from another planet."

"That would be better than being a jerk like you from this planet!" I yelled back.

"Look, guys," Todd said to Adam and Jimmy, "three nerdy nerds. They're so nerdy they don't even know they're nerds." Jimmy and Adam howled with laughter.

"Grow up!" Katie told them.

"There's a ball," Cam said. "Let's go play."

We turned our backs on the three laughing hyenas and ran for the red ball that no one was using. We started bouncing it back and forth to each other. Katie missed and ran to fetch the ball, but Lauren Sanders beat her to it, stopping the ball with her foot. "This is our ball. We're playing with it," she said. Melody, Sherri, and Sarah magically appeared.

"No, you weren't," I said. "It was right over there, and you weren't anywhere around it."

"Oh, look," Lauren said. "It's the nerd talking for the mouse."

"Lauren, are you related to Todd by any chance? You act just like him." I snatched up the ball, and Lauren's foot hit the dirt with a thud that nearly knocked her down. I started bouncing the ball as I ran back to where we had been playing.

"Camilla, you don't really want to play with *them*, do you?" Lauren called.

"Yes, I do!" Cam called back.

"You'll change your mind one day and want to come crawling back to us," Lauren said with her nose in the air again.

"I don't believe I will," Cam answered.

The whistle blew loud and shrill, so we ran to put the ball away and to get in line.

"What a recess!" Katie said.

"What a day!" Camilla said.

"What a life!" I said.

• • •

Ms. Lindell cut social studies short because we were having an awards assembly. Every time we got report cards, we had an assembly. People who got As in reading, spelling, language arts, science, and social studies got a blue ribbon for highest honors. People who got all As and Bs got a red ribbon for honors. PE, art, music, and handwriting didn't count—except that you couldn't flunk them and still get a ribbon.

We all crowded into the multi-purpose room and sat on the floor with our classes. The second and third graders were already there, and the fifth graders were coming in behind us. Since first graders didn't get A, B, C grades, they didn't come. Ms. Lindell crouched down near Todd, so I felt fairly sure he would behave. A few parents sat around the edges of the room, and I saw my mother near the front with her camera on her lap. She got a kick out of these assemblies, and secretly, I was really glad she was there.

Once the fifth graders were seated, Mrs. Peterson held up her hand for everyone to get quiet so she could give her little speech about how hard we all worked and how we have to keep working hard all year. Then she asked the teachers to go up front to read off the names of their honor students. It took a while for the second and third graders to get up and get their ribbons and for everyone to get quiet again. Then it was time for the fourth grade.

Mrs. Sabrinski didn't have anyone for highest honors and had only Sarah Brooks, Mary Garvey, Brenda Queen, Mark Reilly, and John Roberts for honors. Melody didn't even make honors, and she always had before. I was surprised, but then I realized that Sarah was the only one in their crowd that did make honors. I bet Melody's mother was upset.

Ms. Lindell stood to read the names for our class. Somehow she could read and keep one hawk eye on Todd. "I only have one student with highest honors," she said, "and that is Ginger Ryan."

Out of the corner of my eye, I saw Todd's mouth drop open in disbelief. I wished a fly would buzz by and get sucked in. Katie was elbowing me, so I hurried to get to my feet and make my way to the front of the room to shake Mrs. Peterson's hand and to get my blue ribbon. I was kind of embarrassed with everyone looking at me, especially when my mom snapped a picture, but I was proud too. Before I got back to my spot on the floor, Ms. Lindell began reading the names of the kids who got honors. Katie and Cam both got red ribbons, along with about seven other kids. Todd looked shocked to see that Katie, Cam, and I had done so well.

I don't know why he thought we were so stupid. His mouth was still in the Grand Canyon position, and I couldn't resist whispering, "Close your mouth before you suck all the oxygen out of the air." He automatically clamped his mouth closed but didn't say anything. I couldn't believe it. Todd was speechless!

By the time we got back in the classroom, it was time to pack up our book bags and get ready for dismissal. I pulled my notebook and my math and language arts books out of my desk and stuffed them into my book bag. While I wiggled into my jacket, Todd found his voice. "You must have copied off of me."

"Right, Todd. You wish," I said as I stood and pushed my chair under my desk.

"That's why you were standing up there beside her getting a blue ribbon, huh, Todd?" Katie hissed.

"Shut up, you little nerd," Todd said, almost loud enough for Ms. Lindell to hear.

My name was called over the loud speaker to come to the office. Mom was going to take me home. I hurried toward the door. I should have looked down, but I was too anxious to get out of the room, so I didn't see Todd's foot in the aisle. I fell flat on my face and banged my left arm on the desk on the way down. I wanted to cry, but I didn't want Todd to know he had made me cry. He was laughing hysterically. If I hadn't felt so miserable, I would have dug my elbow into the top of his foot.

"Ginger, are you all right?" Ms. Lindell's voice boomed, and everyone looked at me.

I nodded , but really my left arm was throbbing.

"If you tell on me, I'll get you good," Todd hissed.

Through my tears, I saw Ms. Lindell's scruffy brown shoes beside me, so I figured she must have been standing over me. I tried to get up, and Ms. Lindell reached out to help me. I moaned when she grabbed my left arm. "Are you hurt?" I shook my head again, but I don't think she believed me. "What happened?"

"I...I...tripped," I whispered. "M-my mom is waiting." I know my face was beet red. All I wanted was to get out of this miserable classroom and go home.

Mom was waiting for me outside of the office. Her face lit up when she saw me heading toward her. I knew she was proud of me, so I tried to put on a cheerful face. Mom's clever, though. She saw the hurt in my eyes, which were suddenly beginning to fill with tears again. "What's wrong, sweetie?" she asked.

"Nothing."

"I'm so proud of you!" Mom reached to hold my left hand, and I couldn't help pulling away. The tears slid down my cheeks, and I ran for the front door of the school.

"Ginger, what's wrong?" Mom called, running to catch up with me.

I jumped into the car and waited until Mom got in and shut the door before I answered. "I fell down…on…the way out of…the room. I…I hurt m-my arm." Then I started bawling. I just couldn't hold it in any longer.

"Let me see." Mom gently took my left arm and pushed up my sleeve. "It's bruising," she said. "Can you move it? Maybe we should get it x-rayed."

"I-I don't think it's broken," I whispered. I wiggled my arm around a bit. "It just hurts."

"I'm sure it does. I'll go inside and ask for some ice."

"No, Mom. I just want to go home."

During the ride home, I couldn't help wondering how many fourth graders quit school. Maybe I would be the first one. How could I possibly go back into that room tomorrow? Everyone laughed at me. I couldn't face them again. I just couldn't.

When we got home, Mom told me to go to my room and rest, and she put an ice pack on my arm. I couldn't just lie on my bed, though. I got my books out and sat at my desk. I plopped the ice pack back on my left arm and picked up my pencil to do my language arts homework. I sat staring and tapping my pencil when I heard a soft knock at my door.

"Yes?"

The door opened a crack, and Matt stuck his head in. "Can I come in?" he asked. I was too miserable to appreciate the fact that Matt asked before barging in as he usually did.

"Yes."

"What happened, Ginger?"

"Nothing."

"Oh, so that's why you're sitting there in a daze with ice on your arm, because nothing happened." I didn't answer. "It was that Todd kid, wasn't it?" When I still didn't answer, Matt continued. "You should have let me bash his face in, Ginger."

I tried to smile.

"How did you hurt your arm?" Needing to confide in someone, I told Matt, the blabber-mouth.

"Did you tell Mom?" he asked when I had finished.

"No. Don't you say anything either, Matt. You know she would go talk to Ms. Lindell or even Mrs. Peterson, and that would make everything worse."

"How could things get worse, kiddo? Are you going to wait until the little jerk breaks your neck?"

"It's almost Christmas, Matt. Maybe over the break Todd will forget all about tormenting me."

"Right. And maybe elephants will fly. Christmas is a month off, Ginger."

"I'll think of something, Matt. Just please don't say anything to Mom. I told her I tripped and fell, and that's the truth."

"You just forgot to mention that you were tripped on purpose by the big oaf that sits next to you."

"Please, Matt." I hated to beg Matt for favors. I'd probably have to carry out the trash for a month to repay him.

"Okay, Ginger, but I really think you should let me karate chop this guy's head off." Matt grunted, leaped in the air, and waved his hand in his version of a karate chop. "Ow!" he cried when his hand struck the edge of my dresser.

"You'd better forget the karate, Matt," I said, laughing. He left my room rubbing his hurt hand. "Want my ice?" I called.

"Never mind," he mumbled.

chapter 10

Mom made me go back to school, and I tried hard to pretend that nothing happened. At least it was cold out so I could cover my bruised arm with long sleeves. The closer it got to Christmas, the meaner Todd acted toward just about everyone. I didn't know how Adam and Jimmy could stand to be around him. I doubted very seriously that Santa would bring Todd anything for Christmas—not even switches or a lump of coal.

The week before Christmas vacation, Todd was absent for the whole week. Someone said he had the flu. I thought the flu was too good for Todd Ryan. Instead, maybe the earth cracked open and swallowed him alive. That would be better. Or maybe he had moved to Antarctica and turned into a penguin. Whatever the reason, Todd's absence made life more bearable for me. I actually enjoyed the class Christmas party, and I couldn't help being excited because Christmas, my most favorite holiday, was only three days away. I was going to have ten days off from school, ten more days away from Todd—even if I did have to put up with Matt.

• • •

Mom and I cut out cookies in the shape of bells, trees, angels, stars, Santas, and candles and then decorated them with white, green, and red frosting and sprinkles. Of course, I sampled some along the way; they were delicious.

Matt didn't help make cookies; he only helped eat them, but we all decorated the big Christmas tree in the living room. Mom put on the lights and the angel at the top, but Matt and I hung on the ornaments we had collected ever since we were babies. I loved the pine smell the tree gave the room and singing along with the Christmas carols that Mom turned on.

"Can't you hum?" Matt asked, reaching over top of me to hang one of his ornaments.

"Why?" I asked.

"Because you don't know the words, and you sing off-key."

"I do not."

"Yeah, I know you don't know the words."

"I do too."

"Yeah, I know you sing off-key."

"Shut up, Matt."

"That's enough, you two," Mom said just in time. I knew Matt was getting ready to poke me in the ribs with his elbow.

"Let's finish the tree and then have some hot cider," Mom said.

So Matt and I hung the rest of the ornaments in silence. I was hoping for a couple of cookies with my cider.

On Christmas Eve, I played in the snow and wrapped the presents I had gotten Mom and Matt at the Santa's Workshop at school. I played and read and mainly just waited for the day to be over. We went to the eight o'clock church service instead of the late one, and it was all I could do to keep my eyes open during the sermon.

Matt nudged me. "Try to look alive," he said.

I wrinkled up my nose at him to show him I was awake, but then my eyelids became heavy again.

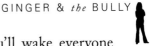

"Don't snore too loud, or you'll wake everyone else up," Matt whispered.

"I'm not asleep."

Mom turned and gave us both a look, so Matt sat back and left me alone.

As soon as we got home from church, I pulled on my red-and-white pajamas that made me look like a giant candy cane and ran to set out milk and cookies for Santa. I brushed my teeth, and Mom tucked me into bed. Then I just lay there. As tired as I was during church, I just couldn't fall asleep. I was excited, but I kept trying to tell myself to calm down. I wanted to go to sleep so the night wouldn't drag on forever.

I must have slept, because the next thing I knew, it was five in the morning. I knew that because the numbers on my clock radio were lit up in red. I couldn't wake Mom up this early, but I couldn't go back to sleep either. Every five minutes I checked the time. Finally it was six—a respectable time to pounce on Mom.

I tiptoed into the dark living room, yanked my stocking off the hook on the mantle, and ran into Mom's room. I jumped onto the bed, crying, "Merry Christmas, Mom!" Mom moaned and wiggled and asked me what time it was. When I told her, she moaned again and tried to pull the covers over her head.

"Come on, Mom. Get up," I pleaded.

She sat up, ran her hands through her hair, and mumbled, "Okay, I'm up." She wrapped her fuzzy blue robe around her, splashed water on her face, and said, "Let's see if Santa came."

I ran back to the living room yelling for Matt to get up. "Pipe down, squirt. It's not even light outside yet."

"Don't you want to open your presents?"

I heard grumbling and bumping and stomping. Then the bear came out of his cave. I ran over and tugged on his arm to get him moving in the direction of the tree and presents.

"Leave me alone," he growled. "I'm coming."

"Merry Christmas to you too, Mr. Scrooge," I said, letting go of his arm and running back to the tree.

Mom shuffled in from the kitchen with her hands wrapped around a mug of coffee. "Oh! Looks like Santa came," she said.

That was all I needed to begin tearing into my presents. I got Felicity, the American Girl doll I wanted, and I got her Christmas dress and her doll.

I got clothes, toys, books, and neat art supplies, but Felicity was my very favorite present. Matt just got dumb stuff like clothes and CDs and movies and a new CD player. He got a few books too, but I could have told Santa that that was a waste. Matt doesn't read. I think it's against his religion. I had almost bought him a crossword puzzle book from the Santa's Workshop, but I figured he would probably just use it as a missile to throw at me at some later time. I settled on a sports trivia water bottle. I thought if he didn't want to read the sports facts he could at least drink from the bottle.

Mom fixed waffles for breakfast. Felicity sat beside me while I ate. I felt kind of bad for Mom. She didn't get many presents. Matt gave her some perfume that smelled like vanilla, and I gave her a coffee mug that said "World's Greatest Mom" on it that I bought at the Santa's Workshop. Matt and I put the rest of our money together to buy her a soft pullover sweater in teal, her favorite color. She said she loved her gifts and gave us each a big hug, but I still wished we could have gotten her more.

• • •

The holidays went by much too fast, and before I knew it, it was New Year's—time to make resolutions and time to go back to school. I thought of all kinds of wild ideas like squirting super glue in Todd's chair so that when it was time for recess he wouldn't be able to get up. Or taking a couple of Matt's dirty socks and gagging Todd with them. Or writing all the wrong answers on my math paper and letting Todd copy them, but I didn't want to get my paper all wrong, and Todd really was doing a good job of flunking all by himself.

Finally I resolved to *try* to be nice to Todd. It would be the hardest thing I'd ever done in my life. I had tried ignoring him, and I had tried saying things back to him. Now I'd try being nice—I'd kill him with kindness. I'd smile and be pleasant. I'd probably throw up. Oh well, I would still have Matt to fight with.

chapter 11

I got the chance to put my plan into action the next morning. Todd's bus was late getting to school, and he stomped into the classroom looking as mad as a hornet.

"Did you have a good Christmas?" I whispered as he struggled to cram his books into his messy desk.

"What's it to you?" he growled.

I shrugged my shoulders then went back to doing the morning work we always did while Ms. Lindell collected lunch and milk money. I could tell that being nice was going to be awfully hard work.

During math, Ms. Lindell called on me to put a problem on the board. I took a deep breath and stood up. This time I saw Todd's foot out in the way. I stepped around it, smiled sweetly at him, and headed for the blackboard. I wanted to stomp on his foot, but my New Year's resolution was still fresh in my mind.

"That's exactly right," Ms. Lindell said when I finished working the problem. Todd didn't have his foot out when I returned to my seat, but he did mimic Ms. Lindell. "That's exactly right, Ginger."

"I don't recall asking for your opinion, Todd." Ms Lindell had heard him. "You do the next problem, please."

Todd stood at the board, wrote down the problem, and stared at it as if the answer would magically appear there. Ms. Lindell gave him a few minutes and then asked Katie to help him. "Perhaps you should pay more attention to your work," Ms. Lindell offered.

We bundled up in coats, hats, and gloves for recess since the weather had gotten even colder than it had been earlier that morning.

"Think you got enough clothes on, Lucretia?" Todd asked as soon as I got outside. "You look like the Goodyear blimp."

"Thanks, Todd," I managed to say without a trace of anger in my voice.

"She's too dumb to know I insulted her." Todd, Jimmy, and Adam laughed.

I ran over to get a jump rope, grinding my teeth so hard I was sure I would wear them down to nubs. I knew if I didn't get as far away from Todd as possible, I would break my resolution.

"You didn't say anything back to the jerk," Katie said, untangling a jump rope.

"I would have punched him in the nose," Cam said. I laughed. Somehow I couldn't picture Cam punching anyone. I told them about my resolution and asked them to help me stick to it.

"We'll try," they agreed. "But it will be awfully hard."

In social studies, Todd was back to drawing his dumb pictures. I just ignored him. Somehow I made it through the rest of the day without saying a mean thing to Todd. One day down, about five and a half *months* to go!

chapter 12

It was almost Valentine's Day. I had been trying to be nice to Todd for over a month now, but a lot of times, it was easier just to ignore him. I had nearly gnawed my tongue off to keep from saying something mean back to him. We were going to have a Valentine's party on Friday. I hoped Todd would be absent.

I helped Mom make chocolate cupcakes with pink icing. We put little heart-shaped candies in the middle of each cupcake. I hoped the kids in my class would like them.

I remembered Valentine's Day when I was five. Daddy had come home from work with presents for each of us. Matt got a box of chocolate candy and a model car to build. I got a heart-shaped box of chocolates with a doll in a beautiful lacy dress attached to the top and a heart-shaped locket . Mom got roses, candy, *and* gold heart earrings. We all danced around and hugged each other until Daddy went off to help Matt build his car. We were so happy.

Now things were different. We were happy again, but it was a different kind of happy. Mom still got us candy and a little present for Valentine's Day, and we always made her cards, but I'm sure she felt a little sad. I always wished we could buy her flowers or something nice like Daddy used to do.

I had addressed cards to all my classmates. Ms. Lindell said that if we were giving out cards, we had to give them to *everyone* in the class. That meant I had to give a card to Todd. I couldn't imagine much worse than giving Todd Ryan a Valentine card.

I took my cupcakes into school on Friday, and Ms. Lindell put them on top of a cabinet, well out of reach, since our party wasn't until two o'clock. We dropped our Valentine cards into the bags we had decorated the day before, and then we did all of our usual morning work. We had to stay inside for recess because it was so cold out, but Ms. Lindell let Katie, Cam, and me go to the media center to work on the computers. Boy, was I glad. Todd seemed in an especially nasty mood, and I didn't want to listen to his mouth all through recess.

At two o'clock, Ms. Lindell let us get our Valentine bags and open our cards. I got all the usual cartoon character cards and the cards with the hearts on them. There was one envelope that didn't have my name written on the outside like the others did. I slid my finger under the flap to open it and pulled out a folded piece of notebook paper. I thought maybe Cam or Katie had written me a letter. I opened the paper, and dirt and dead, dried-up earthworms spilled out on my desk.

"Oooh!" I cried, pushing my chair back and banging it into Katie's desk behind me. Todd began howling with laughter.

"What's wrong?" Katie asked. She leaned around to look and said, "Yuck! Ginger, what's that?"

"The dummy doesn't even know what it is!" Todd slapped his desk and laughed harder.

Then I looked at the paper. Tears came into my eyes, and I couldn't blink them away. I'd recognize that kind of scrawling picture anywhere. Todd had drawn a horrible picture of a car accident with a man, woman, and girl battered and broken up. They were stick figures, and the drawing itself wasn't very good, but it was good enough to upset me. I couldn't stop the tears from sliding down my cheeks.

"Boo hoo!" Todd said. "Lucretia's crying over a picture."

I put my hands over my face, and the picture dropped to the floor. Katie picked it up and yelled, "Todd, you idiot. Don't you know Ginger's dad was killed in a car accident?"

"What's going on?" I heard Ms. Lindell ask.

I couldn't look up at her or anyone else. I jumped out of my chair and ran out of the room. I ran to the far corner of the girls' bathroom, leaned my head against the wall, and cried like a baby. I didn't hear the door open or anyone come into the room—I guess I was crying too hard—but I nearly jumped out of my skin when someone touched me on the shoulder.

"Ginger?" It was Ms. Lindell's voice. "Ginger, I'm sorry. Todd did a very mean thing, and he will be punished for it. I'm sorry he upset you."

"It…it's not your fault," I mumbled.

"It's my fault that I didn't see how much he's been bothering you all year. Katie just explained it to me. Why didn't you tell me?"

I shrugged my shoulders. "I guess I thought he'd get tired of bothering me sooner or later."

"He didn't, though, did he?"

"No," I answered in a small voice. "I thought he'd be meaner if I told on him," I added in an even smaller voice.

Of all things, Ms. Lindell hugged me. It felt really weird at first, but as she patted my back, I began to feel better, and I stopped crying. "Let's go back and have one of those yummy-looking cupcakes you brought."

"I…I can't go in there," I whispered.

"Todd is not in the room, Ginger, and I won't let anyone else say anything."

I believed her. One dirty look from her, and the whole class would be silent forever unless she said to speak. We would probably all stop breathing if she told us to stop. I should have told her about Todd a long time ago. I should have known that she would have made him leave me alone. I could have trusted her. I let her lead me back to class.

Someone had cleaned up the mess at my desk. They had thrown away that awful picture and stacked my Valentines neatly on my desk. It was probably Katie and Cam. All the kids were busy coloring; Ms. Lindell must have told them to draw while she was out of the room. Just like Ms. Lindell said, Todd was nowhere around.

"She yelled at him and sent him to Mrs. Peterson's office," Katie whispered as though she had read my mind.

"Well, class, is everyone ready for cupcakes?" Ms. Lindell asked, still not smiling but trying to sound cheerful. Everyone nodded. Ms. Lindell walked around the room, placing a cupcake on each desk. After putting my cupcake down, she patted my shoulder before moving on to Katie's desk. Kids finally began talking again after being so quiet. Ms. Lindell must have really scared everybody.

"Are you okay?" Katie asked.

"Yeah."

Cam came over to sit at Todd's desk after pretending to spray away the germs. The three of us talked quietly until it was time to go home. I felt like I had been beaten.

• • •

After dinner, Mom gave Matt and me our Valentine candy. She gave Matt a CD he had been wanting and me a fuzzy, white stuffed cat with a red bow tied around its neck. I thanked Mom and hugged her and asked if one day I could have a real cat. She said the stuffed ones were easier to take care of. I had still been in a quiet mood, and Mom picked right up on that.

"Is something wrong, honey?" she asked.

"No."

"Did something happen at school?"

Why are mothers such good mind readers? I started to say no but instead blurted out the whole ugly story. Mom hugged me as tears came into my eyes again.

Matt jumped up with a mean look on his face. "I told you to let me bash his face in a long time ago. Now I'm going to do it. Where does this jerk live?"

All of a sudden I had to laugh. Matt's hair was standing on end, his eyebrows were drawn together in a deep frown, and his nostrils flared. He looked like a mad bull. I expected to see fire shoot out of his nose and ears.

Mom started laughing too. "Calm down, Matthew," she said.

"No, I want to get this kid."

"That won't be necessary, Matt. Maybe I should talk to Ms. Lindell, though."

"That's okay, Mom. Ms. Lindell sent Todd to Mrs. Peterson's office."

• • •

For all my bravery at home, I was kind of scared to go in my classroom at school the next day. I didn't know what Todd would say or do, and I wasn't too eager to find out. I walked as quietly as possible to my seat. I guess I thought that if I were quiet enough, no one would see me either. Todd was now sitting next to Ms. Lindell's desk, so the spot next to me was empty.

Jimmy took the long way to his seat, and when he passed by me, he whispered, "You got Todd in big trouble yesterday. You'll pay." Then he hurried to his seat.

"Todd got himself in trouble," Katie said, leaning forward to speak to me. "Don't worry about them."

I did worry, though. If Todd were anything like my brother, he would figure out a way to get even. Todd didn't come out to recess, much to my relief, and without Todd, Jimmy and Adam were pretty quiet.

Lauren wasn't quiet, though. "I heard you got Todd in trouble," she said.

"Yeah! What a crybaby," Sherri chimed in.

"Can't you take a joke?" Sarah asked.

"Ginger didn't get him in trouble," Katie said. "Todd did something really mean to her, and Ms. Lindell saw. Ginger didn't do anything."

"I'm sure you know everything," Lauren said.

"It's true!" Cam cried.

I was really hurt and angry, and my voice shook a little when I spoke. "Look, Lauren," I said. "I've never done anything to you or your friends here or to Todd or anyone. I can't help it if you don't like me. That's *your* problem. You don't have to come around me, but I happen to like me just fine." I turned to walk away.

"It's a good thing *you* like you!" Lauren shouted and laughed.

"I like her too," Katie said.

"Me too," Cam said.

"Me too," Melody said softly.

Lauren's mouth dropped open in surprise. "Huh?" she said.

"I said I like her too," Melody said in a louder voice. "I'm sorry I've been mean to you all year, Ginger."

"Well, Melody Harper, you can't have it both ways," Lauren said.

"I don't see why I can't like everyone, but if I have to choose, I'd choose Ginger. She's not stuck up like you guys," Melody said. "And even if she doesn't want to be my friend ever again, I don't want to go around being mean anymore."

"Well, be that way!" Lauren said. She, Sarah, and Sherri stomped off with their noses in the air.

"We could always hope for rain," Melody said, and we all laughed. Melody played ball with Cam, Katie, and me for the rest of recess.

chapter 13

Life was a little better since I no longer sat next to Todd. I didn't have to worry about someone drawing dumb pictures of me. I didn't have to hide my papers to keep someone from cheating off of me. I didn't have to worry about tripping over someone's big foot in the aisle. Three days a week, Todd spent recess with Mrs. Carter, the counselor, and on the other two days, Cam, Katie, and I worked in the library. On the days we went outside, Melody played with us. I didn't think Melody would ever be my best friend again. A best friend wouldn't be mean to you or turn against you. A best friend would stick by you in the bad times like Katie and Cam did. But

Melody was a general friend even if she wasn't a close one anymore.

I was still working really hard on my schoolwork. I still hadn't gotten an A in handwriting yet, no matter how neatly I tried to write. I figured Ms. Lindell probably didn't believe in giving someone *all* As, but I'd keep trying.

Spring was back at last, and I signed up to play soccer on a neighborhood team. We practiced two evenings a week. I enjoyed running up and down the field. Every now and then I got to actually kick the ball. Of course, Matt the Brat always had to give me advice. He thinks he knows everything about soccer too. He walks me home from practices because his team practices on the same nights.

"The idea of the game is to kick the ball, Ginger."

"I know, Matt."

"Then why don't you kick it?"

"I would if the dumb boys would stop hogging the ball all the time."

"Don't let the boys scare you. Get in there and kick."

"I'd like to kick you right now, Matt."

"Hey, I'm just trying to help."

"Thanks a lot."

Matt made me practice with him at home on the nights we didn't practice with our teams. I surprised myself, and I think I surprised Matt too. I could almost outrun him. Of course, whenever I caught up to him, he'd pretend he got a bad leg cramp that slowed him down. Really, he just couldn't admit that I was a fast runner—almost as fast as he was. Me, a girl, and a much younger girl at that!

On the day of my first game, Mom walked with us to the park. I hoped Matt's game would be at the same time as mine so he wouldn't be able to watch me play. I wasn't that lucky, though. Matt's game was right after mine. He would sit on the bleachers and make a mental note of every mistake I made, and he would share each and every one of these with me on the way home. I couldn't wait.

My team warmed up a little, and then I trotted over to take a sip from the water bottle Mom held for me. The other team ran out onto the field to warm up, and I suddenly felt my stomach drop to my feet. "Oh no," I moaned.

"What's wrong?" Mom asked.

"That's Todd, Jimmy, and Adam on the other team. I can't play. Take me home, Mom, please!" I begged.

"Which ones? I'll knock all their heads together and then punch their lights out," Matt said and started to stand up.

Mom's firm hand on his leg made him stop with his behind off the bleachers in midair. "You'll do no such thing, Matthew. Now sit down."

Matt's behind lowered back onto the bleachers. "Aw, come on, Mom," he whined.

"Ginger, you go on out and play your best," Mom said, ignoring Matt but keeping her hand on his leg just in case. "Don't let those boys keep you from playing."

"Yeah, squirt," Matt chimed in. "Go out there and run faster than you've ever run. Take the ball away from them, but don't let them take it from you. Show them you're the best soccer player and they'd better not mess with you. You can do it."

I couldn't believe Matt's confidence in me or my soccer-playing ability, but it gave me more confidence in myself. I'd show them I wasn't scared of them. I ran over to my coach as he was getting ready to give us our positions. I was going to play front line—wing position. I'd be able to run down the field and even score if I were very lucky.

We lined up on the field, and at the referee's whistle, the game began. Todd played on the front line for his team, but Jimmy was a halfback, and Adam was the goalie. I had a vision of myself taking the ball away from Todd, racing downfield, and kicking the ball over Adam's head to score. *Dream on, Ginger*, I said to myself.

For the first few minutes of the game, the ball never came near me. Then I got the chance to kick the ball down the sideline, but I passed to one of the boys in the middle so he could score for us. Later, I had the ball and was clear to score. I took aim the best that I could and kicked with all my might. Adam caught the ball, so I didn't score.

"Ha! Ha! You didn't make it, Lucretia!" he yelled. That made me more determined to score a goal.

On the next play, Todd was kicking the ball. In the distance, I could hear Matt's big mouth. "Take the ball, Ginger! Don't let him get down the field!" Todd and I were both kicking at the ball. He missed the ball and kicked me on the leg, but it didn't hurt because I had on shin guards. I quickly kicked the ball away with my other foot and outran Todd down the field. I tried to score, but Adam caught the ball again.

Before I knew it, the whistle blew for halftime. "Great game!" my coach said as I ran off the field. I reached for an orange slice—our half-time snack—but a larger hand clamped around my wrist before I could get a juicy piece of orange out of the big plastic bowl.

"What?" I began.

"Come here, Ginger," Matt said, pulling me away from the oranges.

"Wait, Matt, I want an orange."

He grabbed a slice, stuffed it in my mouth, and jerked me away from everyone else. "You're playing a super game, squirt. If you want to score, you've got to stop kicking the ball straight at the chump goalie. He'll catch it every time. You've either got to kick it over his head, which would be hard to do, or kick to the side of him—something to catch him off guard."

"Oh, great. That sure sounds easy," I wailed.

"It won't be that hard. Just watch for your chance." Matt offered a few more words of wisdom before letting go of my arm so I could get a drink of water before the second half of the game.

The ref blew his shrill whistle again for the second half of the game to begin, so I raced out to my position on the front line. I was glad the coach hadn't changed me. I wanted so badly to score a goal. I crossed my fingers for luck. I would have crossed my toes too, but I didn't think I'd be able to run very well like that.

I did a good job of getting the ball away from the other team and getting it to some of my teammates. I outran almost everyone, even Todd, so I felt pretty good about myself. My team was ahead four to one, but I still wanted to score a goal. Todd tripped some boy on my team, so we got a penalty kick and scored another goal. We were beating them good, but I still *had* to score.

The ball rolled in my direction. I outran Todd but then had to face Jimmy. I ran close to him and then swerved away at the last second so he couldn't kick the ball away from me. Faintly I heard, "Go, Ginger!" in the background. Then I heard, "Shoot, Ginger!"

I was close to the goal. Adam had that know-it-all look on his face. "Come on, Lucretia!" he yelled. "I'm ready. I'll catch it again." I kicked the ball to the side of the goal. Adam dashed over, and just when he bent down to grab it, I booted the ball over his head and scored a goal.

"Yes!" I shouted, jumping up and down.

"Way to go, squirt!" I heard Matt yell. I wished he wouldn't call me "squirt."

Adam had a look of pure disbelief on his face. He sure hadn't expected me to score a goal. Just then the whistle blew. The game was over. I had just made it. If the game had ended a minute earlier, I wouldn't have scored. The parents were clapping and cheering as we all ran off the field. Now we had to go out and shake hands with the members of the other team. I just knew that Todd would spit on his hand before he shook mine, so I was in no hurry to get in line.

We all trotted onto the field in single file to meet the other team. To my complete surprise, Todd gave me a high-five and said, "Good game, Ginger." I nearly dropped my teeth. Then Jimmy and Adam said, "Yeah, good game." My hand wasn't wet and slimy, and the three terrors of Chestnut Ridge had said something nice to me. What a shock!

When we got off the field, the coach told us how proud he was of us and all the usual junk coaches say. Mom hugged me, and Matt patted me on the head—pounded me on the head was more like it.

"Ow," I said. "Lighten up, will you?"

"Sorry, squirt."

"And don't call me squirt."

"Sorry! Boy, the kid scores a goal and thinks she's a queen or something."

I could tell Matt was proud of me, though. Maybe the walk home after his game wouldn't be so bad after all.

chapter 14

The school year was almost over, and I had been feeling better about life lately. Melody was my friend again—not my best friend because that spot was taken by Katie and Cam—but she was a friend. I had been doing a good job on my schoolwork and had been working extra hard on my handwriting.

One day at the end of May, Mrs. Carter, the counselor, called me into her office at recess. It would be one of the days that Todd spent recess with her! I wasn't looking forward to recess.

"Come in, Ginger," Mrs. Carter called when I knocked at her open door. I could see that Todd was already sitting in her office, and I felt my legs go stiff.

They didn't want to carry me into that room with Todd. "Come on in," Mrs. Carter said a little louder this time. I guess she thought I was hard of hearing.

I stepped into the room and sat on the chair Mrs. Carter told me to sit on. I held my hands in my lap and picked at my fingernails.

"Ginger, Todd and I felt that you should know some things that may explain why he has been so mean to you this year. He asked me to tell you, but he wanted to be here too. Okay?"

I nodded because I couldn't get any words to come out.

Mrs. Carter told me a whole bunch of stuff but ended with, "So you see, Ginger, when Todd's father left the family last summer without any warning, Todd felt hurt, scared, and very angry. He assumed that you had a father and mother like he used to have, and since your last names were the same, he took all his anger out on you. Maybe he thought his dad had gone to live with you or maybe he was just mad because you were a Ryan and you had a father. At least he thought you did. He didn't know your dad died. Anyway, we're still working on Todd's problems, but he wanted you to know this. Do you want to say anything, Todd?"

"I, well, I'm sorry I did all those stupid things."

I'm sure my mouth must have dropped open because I felt my throat get all dry. How dare Todd blame me for his father leaving! How dare he make my life so miserable just because my last name is the same as his! How dare—

I closed my mouth and tried to swallow. How could Todd's dad just leave him? My dad didn't want to leave me; he had loved me. Todd's dad *chose* to leave. Poor Todd.

What? I couldn't believe I felt sorry for Todd, but I really did. I've been without a dad for four years, so I'm kind of used to him being gone. Todd is just learning what it's like to be without a dad.

Todd and Mrs. Carter stared at me, waiting for me to respond to Todd's apology. I didn't know what I should feel or say. Everything was jumbled up inside my head. I shrugged my shoulders and mumbled, "I lived through it."

"Why don't you both go out for recess? We'll meet again day after tomorrow, Todd."

I jumped up and headed for the door as fast as I could. Todd was a little ways behind me.

"Hey, Ginger," he called. "Where did you learn how to play soccer like that?"

I couldn't believe he had called me Ginger instead of Lucretia. I thought that time on the soccer field had been my imagination playing tricks on me. "My big brother practices with me."

"You're a good player," he said before running out the door to join his friends on the playground.

"Thanks," I said, but I didn't know if he heard me.

• • •

The last day of school was hot and miserable. At least it was a half day. We were having another awards assembly at nine o'clock to give out ribbons and awards for the last marking period. The first graders came to this assembly, and it took almost forever for the teachers to give out awards for everything from math to handwriting to finally learning how to sit in the seat all day.

At last it was time for the fourth grade teachers to give out their awards. Mrs. Sabrinski still didn't have anyone who got all As, but Melody got all As and B's this time, so I'm sure she was happy. Her mother would probably be even happier.

Ms. Lindell, wearing the same lavender skirt and flowered shirt she had worn when I had first met her at the open house before the school year began last fall, walked to the front of the multi-purpose room to hand out her awards.

"I have two people who earned highest honors this marking period," she said. "First is Katie Stevens."

I clapped loudly because I knew how hard Katie had worked. Suddenly, though, a chill went through me. If Ms. Lindell were going in alphabetical order, she had already passed my name. My heart thumped so hard that I almost didn't hear what Ms. Lindell was saying.

"My other student earned As in all of the subjects—even handwriting, art, music, and PE," Ms. Lindell said. "This person has also had highest honors all year. Ginger Ryan."

Cam elbowed me and whispered, "Good job!" I leaped to my feet and made my way to the front of the room. Ms. Lindell shook my hand, handed me a blue ribbon, and smiled—a real smile with teeth showing and everything. No kidding! I held my breath waiting for lightning to strike. I jumped when I saw a sudden flash of light and then grinned at my mother, who had just snapped a picture of Ms. Lindell smiling at me. I gave Ms. Lindell a huge smile before looking out to see everyone in the room clapping for me.